Raggedy Ann & Andy Giant Treasury

This Book
Belongs
to

_____

Raggedy Ann & Andy Giant Treasury

4 Adventures plus 12 Short Stories
Adapted from:

Raggedy Ann's Wishing Pebble • *Raggedy Ann and Andy and the Camel with the Wrinkled Knees* • *Raggedy Ann in the Snow White Castle* • *Raggedy Ann and the Hobby Horse* • *Raggedy Ann in the Deep Deep Woods* • *Raggedy Ann and the Happy Meadow* • *Marcella: A Raggedy Ann Story*

by Johnny Gruelle

Retold by Nancy Golden
Foreword by Corey Nash

DERRYDALE BOOKS
New York

The adventures and stories in RAGGEDY ANN & ANDY GIANT TREASURY have been retold from the original books as follows:

Raggedy Ann & Andy's Wishing Pebble and *Mr. Muskrat & Timothy Turtle* adapted from RAGGEDY ANN'S WISHING PEBBLE; *Raggedy Ann & Andy in the Land of the Loonies* adapted from RAGGEDY ANN & ANDY AND THE CAMEL WITH THE WRINKLED KNEES; *Raggedy Ann & Andy in the Snow White Castle* adapted from RAGGEDY ANN IN THE SNOW WHITE CASTLE; *Raggedy Ann & Andy and the Hobby Horse* adapted from RAGGEDY ANN AND THE HOBBY HORSE; *The Picnic, Squeakie,* and *"Shipwrecked"* adapted from MARCELLA: A RAGGEDY ANN STORY; *A Kitty Trick, The Fairy Ring, Ice Cream Sodas for All!, Two Soft Brown Eyes,* and *The Hootieowl Party* adapted from RAGGEDY ANN IN THE DEEP DEEP WOODS; *Hinkie-Dinkie, The Fairies' Cure,* and *The Brownie's Kiss* adapted from RAGGEDY ANN AND THE HAPPY MEADOW.

Published 1984 by Derrydale Books, distributed by Crown Publishers, Inc., 225 Park Avenue South, New York, New York 10003, by arrangement with The Bobbs-Merrill Company, Inc.

Manufactured in the United States of America

Library of Congress Cataloging in Publication Data

Golden, Nancy.
    Raggedy Ann & Andy giant treasury.

    "Adapted from Raggedy Ann's wishing pebble, Raggedy Ann and Andy and the camel with the wrinkled knees, Raggedy Ann in the snow white castle, Raggedy Ann and the hobby horse, Raggedy Ann in the deep deep woods, Raggedy Ann and the happy meadow, Marcella: a Raggedy Ann story, by Johnny Gruelle."
    Summary: Ms. Golden presents her adaptations of several Raggedy Ann and Andy stories.
    1. Children's stories, American. [1. Dolls — Fiction.   2. Short Stories]
I. Gruelle, Johnny, 1880?–1938. II. Title. III. Title: Raggedy Ann and Andy giant treasury.
PZ8.9.G657Rag 1984   [E]   84-17654
ISBN: 0-517-455943
Book design by Deirdre Ingersoll Newman
h g f e d c

Contents

Foreword

Who would have thought that a red-headed rag doll with shoe-button eyes and a candy heart would capture the hearts of millions of readers? But she did. According to legend, Raggedy Ann was originally fashioned from a rag doll belonging to Johnny Gruelle's mother. She was "born" in print more than half a century ago and continues to enchant young and old alike to this day.

Gruelle invented the first Raggedy Ann stories to entertain his young daughter Marcella, who then possessed the rag doll. Later, he illustrated these stories and had them published. The demand for Raggedy Ann stories was so great that two years later her rag brother Raggedy Andy appeared. And the rest is history. Johnny Gruelle, collaborating with his son, Worth, and his brother, Justin, went on to write and illustrate approximately forty Raggedy Ann and Raggedy Andy books, seven of which have been delightfully retold by Nancy Golden for this *Giant Treasury*.

The four adventures and twelve short stories included here contain more than 150 full-color illustrations and present Raggedy Ann and Raggedy Andy at their lovable best. Follow them through the Happy Meadow and into the deep deep woods as they meet all kinds of wonderful, wacky characters—from the Camel with the Wrinkled Knees to Witch Wiggle to the King of the Loonies!

Johnny Gruelle once said, "It does pay to do more work than you are paid for after all. Someone usually sees it sometime and appreciates it." Which, of course, is an understatement in the case of Raggedy Ann and Raggedy Andy. As this *Giant Treasury* shows, there is much to appreciate in these pages. I hope you will enjoy it as much as I have and will continue to share and treasure these wonderful stories and illustrations for generations to come.

Corey Nash

New York City
1984

Introduction

Raggedy Ann and Raggedy Andy are two little rag dolls stuffed with nice white cotton, with bright shoe-button eyes and cheery, happy smiles painted on their rag faces.

Raggedy Ann and Raggedy Andy are very happy little creatures, too, and they have had so much fun in their raggedy lives, they just can't help being joyous and kindly.

Raggedy Andy always says, "The reason Raggedy Ann is so lovable and kindly and generous and able to think so nicely is that she has a candy heart with the words 'I love you,' printed on it"; but Raggedy Andy is just as kindly and cheery and generous as dear Raggedy Ann, and he has no candy heart.

And maybe it is just as Raggedy Ann has often said to the other dolls in the nursery: "If one just thinks nice, kindly things, if one just does generous, helpful deeds, then that person is filled with a thrill of happiness that shines right through even the shabbiest clothes and brings loving friends close by."

Adventures

Raggedy Ann & Andy's Wishing Pebble

Finding the Magic Wishing Pebble

One day Raggedy Ann and Raggedy Andy were lying along the edge of Looking Glass Brook.

"I wish that we could find a Wishing Pebble!" said Raggedy Andy. "We could wish for so many nice things."

"Do you know what a Wishing Pebble looks like?" asked Raggedy Ann.

"Well, I don't think I have ever seen one," Raggedy Andy replied, "but I have heard that they are round and smooth and very white."

"Is this one, do you suppose?" Raggedy Ann asked as she held up a white pebble.

"Well," said Raggedy Andy, "it *looks* like one, but I know how we can be sure."

"Let's wish for something and see if it comes true!" said Raggedy Ann.

"Let's wish for something for Mr. and Mrs. Muskrat," Raggedy Andy suggested.

"That's a wonderful idea," said Raggedy Ann.

"I'll wish for the Muskrats to have a magic ice cream soda fountain in their living room!" Raggedy Ann said.

And Raggedy Ann closed her eyes and wished.

"Now let's run to the Muskrats' house and see if our wish came true!" cried Raggedy Andy.

Just then they saw Freddy Fieldmouse running toward them.

"Guess what?" Freddy Fieldmouse asked the Raggedys.

"Tell us!" cried the Raggedys.

"Well," said Freddy Fieldmouse, "I was walking by the Muskrats' house when I heard Mrs. Muskrat squeal."

"Oh, my, what happened?" asked Raggedy Andy.

"Well," said Freddy Fieldmouse, "I went inside their house to see if she was all right, and what do you think?"

"What?" the Raggedys asked together.

"Well, there in the living room stood Mr. and Mrs. Muskrat, and they were drinking ice cream sodas from their new soda fountain!"

Raggedy Ann and Raggedy Andy jumped up and down and danced about.

"Where do you think the soda fountain came from?" Raggedy Ann asked, winking at Raggedy Andy.

"Mrs. Muskrat told me that they heard a strange noise coming from the living room, so Mr. Muskrat picked up a stick and went inside to look.

"They certainly were surprised to find that the noise was coming from a soda fountain!

"Now I'm going to invite everyone to the Muskrats' house for ice cream sodas!" said Freddy Fieldmouse, and off he ran.

"I guess we must have found a real Wishing Pebble after all," said Raggedy Andy.

"I wish that I had kept it," said Raggedy Ann. "I thought it was only makebelieve, so I buried it in the sand again."

"Well, we had fun with it, anyway!" Raggedy Andy laughed. "Now let's go over to the Muskrats' home and see their new soda fountain!"

The Soda Fountain Comes and Goes

"You are just in time," Mrs. Muskrat cried out as the two Raggedys arrived. Then she handed each of them an ice cream soda.

Soon all the neighbors began to arrive.

Raggedy Ann told them all about the Wishing Pebble and that she had buried it in the sand.

"Why don't we try to find the pebble together?" suggested Mr. Muskrat, and out they all went to look for the Wishing Pebble.

They searched and searched along Looking Glass Brook, but they could not find it. By then everyone was quite thirsty, so they went back to the Muskrat house for ice cream sodas.

"Oh dear me," Mrs. Muskrat cried when she walked into the living room. "The magic soda fountain is gone!"

"Ha! Ha! Ha!" a voice said. "Of course it's gone!"

"Who is that?" Raggedy Andy shouted.

Mrs. Muskrat began to cry.

"I saw Raggedy Ann bury the Magic Wishing Pebble," the voice said, "and I took it! Now I have the magic soda fountain!"

"I wonder who that is!" Raggedy Andy said.

"If I find him, I shall throw him down and take the pebble away from him!" said Georgie Groundhog.

"We mustn't do that!" said Raggedy Ann. "For you know the Magic Wishing Pebble really belongs to whoever finds it. And because I buried it, it belonged to whoever found it next."

"Then how can we ever get it back?" Henrietta Hedgehog asked.

"Well," said Raggedy Ann, "we must find out who has the pebble. Then if he loses it, or buries it, as I did, we can find it again."

"First we had better find out who has the Wishing Pebble," said Raggedy Andy. "And we'll never know by sitting here!"

They all ran out the door.

Searching for the Wishing Pebble

When Raggedy Ann and Raggedy Andy left the Muskrats' house, they walked down the bank of Looking Glass Brook asking all they met if they knew who had found the Wishing Pebble.

As they walked on, they met Grampy Hoppytoad, and they asked him about the Wishing Pebble.

"I'm afraid I don't know who has it," Grampy Hoppytoad said. "But I will keep my two large goggle eyes open." Then he shook hands goodbye with the Raggedys and waddled off.

Raggedy Ann and Raggedy Andy walked on along the brook until they came upon Clifton Crawdad, sticking out of a little hole in the sand.

"Have you seen someone with a Wishing Pebble?" asked Raggedy Ann, and she told Clifton Crawdad all about the Wishing Pebble and the Muskrats' ice cream soda fountain.

"I know who has it," Clifton Crawdad said. "It's Minky, and he's very selfish and unkind!"

"Indeed he must be," said Raggedy Andy.

"Well, if I see him again, I will be sure to tell you," said Clifton Crawdad.

"I'm right here!" cried a voice from behind the weeds. "And I want to know why my Wishing Pebble isn't working."

"It worked very nicely when I had it," said Raggedy Ann.

"You can't fool me!" the voice cried. "I know you have a candy heart, and that's the reason the pebble worked so well for you!"

"That's not the reason at all!" Raggedy Ann laughed. "It would work just as well for you if you would wish unselfish things."

"You just wait!" cried the voice. "I'll show you!"

And Raggedy Ann and Raggedy Andy saw a strange little creature run out of the weeds and go scampering away.

The Raggedys Meet Mr. Minky

"Mr. Minky is certainly a selfish man," Raggedy Andy said, as they walked through the woods.

"Ha! Ha! Ha!" laughed a voice from a tree nearby.

Looking up, whom should the Raggedys see but Mr. Minky with a fishing pole and line.

"How do you expect to catch any fish in the tall grass, Mr. Minky?" Raggedy Ann asked.

"Oh, I'm not fishing for fish!" Mr. Minky said with a sly wink.

The Raggedys walked over to the tree and looked in the grass to see what Mr. Minky was fishing for.

"Hee! Hee! Hee!" Minky chuckled as he gave the line a jerk.

The hook caught on Raggedy Ann's apron and then on Raggedy Andy's pants, and then the two rag dolls hung in the air, twisting and twirling.

"Now that I have you two rag dolls, I know the Wishing Pebble will work, and I will wish for all kinds of things for myself."

But Mr. Minky did not see Bertha Bumblebee sitting behind him. Bertha buzzed around Minky, and then stung him right on his head.

Minky jumped to his feet, dropping the fishing pole with the two Raggedys attached, leaped out of the tree, and ran off yowling.

"Thank you," said Raggedy Ann and Raggedy Andy. Bertha Bumblebee winked at the Raggedys and then flew away.

As the Raggedys walked along, they met Winnie Woodchuck. They told her the story of Minky and the Wishing Pebble.

"Why don't you rest for a while and have some tea and cookies with Walter Woodchuck and me?" Winnie Woodchuck suggested.

So they all went back to the Woodchuck house, where Walter Woodchuck was sitting on the front step waiting.

The four of them sat in front of the fire, and for a little while they forgot all about Mr. Minky.

All of a sudden the door opened, and without even knocking, in walked Minky.

"I'll have a cup of that tea, and some cookies, too!" he said.

"Now you just march right out, Mr. Minky!" Winnie Woodchuck said. "You are very rude!"

"You'd better be very careful about what you call me!" Minky said. "I have a magical Wishing Pebble!"

"Wishing Pebble or not, you cannot be rude in my house!" Winnie Woodchuck said, and she took her broom and chased Minky out the door.

"You won't get the Magic Wishing Pebble away from me, anyway!" Minky cried as he ran down the road.

"Minky is a very unpleasant fellow," said Winnie Woodchuck.

"Yes, he is," agreed Raggedy Andy. "And I think it's time for us to be on our way."

"Thank you very much for the tea and cookies," Raggedy Ann said. "We hope we will see you again soon."

Mr. Minky Gets All Wet

After the Raggedys left the Woodchuck home they walked to Looking Glass Brook.

There upon a log sat Minky, fishing.

All of a sudden, Minky's pole gave a big jerk, and before he could catch himself, he was pulled into the water.

Raggedy Andy got a long stick and held it out so Minky could catch hold of it. Then the two Raggedys pulled Minky ashore.

"That settles it!" Minky said when he could catch his breath.

"Settles what?" Raggedy Andy asked.

"You Raggedys just saved my life. And now I know that it was wrong of me to take the Wishing Pebble and make the soda fountain disappear from the Muskrats' home."

Raggedy Ann looked at Minky and smiled.

"Yes sir," Minky said, "I am so very, very, very—" Then Minky's eyes filled with tears, and he began crying loudly.

"The Wishing Pebble is really yours, Raggedy Ann," Minky said, and he put the small white stone in her hand. "I am very sorry that I have been so mean. Now you take the pebble and make a lot of nice lovely wishes with it!"

"Thank you, Mr. Minky," Raggedy Ann said. "You are a kind man after all."

Then she and Raggedy Andy shook hands with Minky, and watched him as he sadly walked away.

"I expect Mr. Minky will be shouting with joy when he gets to his home," Raggedy Ann said.

"What makes you think so?" asked Raggedy Andy.

"Because I have already wished that there will be a lollipop garden right outside his kitchen porch," said Raggedy Ann.

"Now Mr. Minky can find out just how much fun it will be

having his friends help him enjoy the nice things he has!" said Raggedy Andy.

Saving the Wishing Pebble

"The first thing I'm going to do," said Raggedy Ann, "is wish for a new soda fountain for the Muskrats." And then she closed her eyes and wished.

"Let's run over there and see if your wish came true!" cried Raggedy Andy, as he caught her hand and ran toward the Muskrat house.

Mr. Muskrat was out on the bank of Looking Glass Brook, calling through a megaphone: "Everyone is invited to the Muskrat home—we are having a grand party! Hurry and come!"

And all around the meadow creatures and the woods folk were flying, running, and wiggling toward the Muskrat home.

Everyone crowded around the Raggedys and listened to the story of how they had recovered the Magic Wishing Pebble.

Then Raggedy Ann took out her handkerchief, unfolded it, and showed the Wishing Pebble to everyone.

"I do hope I don't lose it," said Raggedy Ann.

"I hope so too," said Raggedy Andy.

"I have an idea!" Mrs. Muskrat cried as she ran into her bedroom. She came out with a sewing basket.

"I will sew the Wishing Pebble into your body, just like your candy heart. Then you will never lose it!"

And that is just what Mrs. Muskrat did.

Raggedy Ann kissed Mrs. Muskrat and thanked her.

"I guess our adventure is at an end!" Raggedy Andy said. "For Raggedy Ann and I must return home, and we have a long way to go."

"Is there any other nice thing I could wish for you, Mrs. Muskrat?" Raggedy Ann asked.

"Dear me, no, Raggedy Ann!" Mrs. Muskrat replied. "What more could we wish for than to make our friends happy?"

Raggedy Ann & Andy in the Land of the Loonies

The Camel with the Wrinkled Knees

Raggedy Ann and Raggedy Andy sat under a tree, watching the sun shine its rays through the woods. "Isn't it beautiful!" Raggedy Ann said.

"It certainly is," said a voice from behind the tree.

Out walked a strange-looking creature. It was a Camel, made out of flannel and stuffed with sawdust.

His legs were so wrinkled that it seemed he might fall forward with each step.

And when he tried to sit down next to Raggedy Ann and Raggedy Andy, his knees gave way and he rolled over onto his side.

"My legs are not what they used to be." The Camel laughed. "See how wrinkled my knees are?"

When Raggedy Andy tried to smooth them out, the Camel smiled and said, "It doesn't do a bit of good. The wrinkles come right back in again just as soon as I stand up."

"Where are you off to, Mr. Camel?" Raggedy Andy asked.

"Well, you see, last night I came upon a little girl who was stuck in a field of Snap Dragons. I could not help her myself, so I told her I would find someone who could."

"Maybe we could help," said Raggedy Andy.

"Oh, that would be wonderful," said the Camel, "but now I cannot remember where the poor little girl was! You see, it was dark when I found her, and now in the daylight nothing looks familiar."

"I have an idea!" said Raggedy Ann. "If we blindfold you, it will be just the same as if it were dark, and then you could retrace your steps."

"What a fine idea!" said the Camel.

And so Raggedy Ann put her handkerchief over the Camel's eyes. Then she and Raggedy Andy jumped on the Camel's back, and they went off through the woods in search of the little girl.

Jenny

"I think I see the little girl over there!" Raggedy Ann cried, and sure enough she did.

The Camel immediately stopped, and Raggedy Ann and Raggedy Andy rolled off his back and into the grass.

"Don't come any closer, or the Snap Dragons will catch you!" the little girl cried.

But the Raggedys had already run over to her. "Catch hold of our hands and we will run away from here," said Raggedy Andy.

It was too late. The Snap Dragons had also fastened themselves around the Raggedys' legs, and nobody could move.

"I wonder how long we will have to stay here before we are rescued," Raggedy Ann said.

"We may have to stay here years and years!" the little girl cried. Then she told Raggedy Ann and Raggedy Andy all about herself.

"My name is Jenny," the little girl began, "and my brother's name is Jan. We live in a little cottage right here in the center of the woods."

"Where is Jan now?" Raggedy Andy asked.

"Well," said Jenny, "one day the queerest little man-creature came into our house.

"It was a Loonie!

"He had large rolling eyes and a long red nose and crooked legs. He was so funny-looking that Jan and I had to laugh, which made the Loonie very angry.

"All at once, the Loonie caught Jan's feet and dragged him out of the cottage and away through the woods!

"I looked and looked but I could not find them. Then when I walked across this field of Snap Dragons, they twined around my feet and I could not move." And with that Jenny began to cry again.

"Please do not cry," Raggedy Ann begged. "We will help you find Jan."

The Tired Old Horse

All at once from out of the woods, a funny old Horse appeared.

"Why is everyone standing around?" the Horse asked. "Is there going to be a parade?"

"My friends there have been captured by a field of Snap Dragons," said the Camel.

"Hmmm," the Horse said, "I will look into this."

The Horse walked right up to Jenny and looked at her through his spectacles. "I know

you," he cried. "You used to live in the little cottage in the woods, didn't you?"

"Why, yes," Jenny replied. "How did you know?"

"Well," the old Horse said, "my master used to drive me through the woods every day, hauling wood. And that's where I'd see you and Jan. But what are you doing here?"

"Jenny has been captured by the Snap Dragons," Raggedy Andy said, "and so have we, and now so have you!"

"Nonsense!" The old Horse laughed. "I shall just have to eat a path out of here."

And without another word, the Horse started eating, and in a short time they were all able to walk away and sit down beside the Camel.

"Now what shall we do about Jan?" Jenny asked.

"I think I know," said the Horse. "You see, I saw the Loonie come out of your little cottage dragging Jan. I wanted to rescue Jan, but I could not do so, because I was hitched to the cart.

"But I watched until I saw the Loonie take Jan inside a great tree, and I'll bet I can show you where it is."

"Then let's all go look!" Raggedy Andy cried, as he jumped to his feet.

So Jenny climbed up on the Horse's back, and Raggedy Ann and Raggedy Andy climbed on top of the Camel.

And off they went in search of Jan.

The Land of the Loonies

The Camel and the Horse raced across the fields. In a few moments they came to a great tree.

"This is where the Loonie took Jan," the Horse said.

"But how could the Loonie drag Jan into the tree when there isn't a single hole in it?" Raggedy Andy asked, as he walked around the tree.

"Mmmm," the Horse said, scratching his head. "This must be a magic tree, or at the least the entrance into the tree is covered with magic so we are unable to see it. Perhaps if the Camel couldn't see at all, he might be able to find it."

So Raggedy Ann again blindfolded the Camel. And when they had all crowded around and caught hold of his nose, the Camel backed into the tree and they disappeared inside.

A wonderful sight met their eyes. There in the distance stood a beautiful castle.

All at once, they were surrounded by Loonies, who marched them into the castle and up to the King of the Loonies.

"Aha!" the Loonie King cried. "What have we captured?"

"Prisoners," replied a Loonie Guard on a hobby horse.

"I can see that!" the Loonie King said. "But why are they here in the Land of the Loonies?"

"We have come in search of Jan," Raggedy Ann replied. "One of the Loonies carried him away, and we have come to find him."

"Hmmm," the Loonie King mused as he scratched his head. "I suppose you will have to answer one of my riddles."

"Do you mean that if we answer the riddle, you will let Jan go with us?" Raggedy Ann asked.

"Yes," the King replied. "And now I shall ask you the riddle—as soon as I've thought of one."

Everyone waited while the King was deep in thought.

The King's Riddle

"Oh!" the King finally said. "I've just thought of a good riddle! How can a hobgoblin hobble a gobble? There's a hard one."

"That's not a riddle at all!" Raggedy Ann whispered. "He's just making it up."

"I think so too," said the Horse. "So let's just make up an answer!"

Raggedy Ann turned to the King and said, "The hobgoblin can hobble a gobble by gobbling the hobble with a goghoblin."

"Good!" the King cried. "I mean, bad, for I did not wish you to guess the answer. Now I will have to ask you another riddle."

"Oh, that isn't fair," Raggedy Ann said. "You promised that if we answered the riddle you would let Jan go, so it wouldn't be fair if you did not keep your promise!"

"Boo! Boo!" Raggedy Andy shouted at the King.
All at once the King began to cry.

"You are all good and fair and kind," sobbed the Loonie King. "But I have not been, have I?"

Raggedy Ann shook her head no.

"Well then, I shall let Jan go," the King said.

When Jan arrived, he hugged and kissed everyone.

"That was very good and fair and kind of you," Raggedy Ann said to the King, and she gave him a kiss.

Then the friends marched out of the castle, down the valley, and back through the magic tree.

When they came out into the woods, Raggedy Ann said, "Raggedy Andy and I must be getting home."

"I suppose we should be wandering on, too," the Horse said to the Camel.

"Jan and I would love for you and the Camel to come live with us," Jenny said.

"Oh, we would love that!" the Horse and the Camel cried.

"I am so glad," said Raggedy Ann. "For you know, the best kind of happiness is the kind you share with your friends."

Raggedy Ann & Andy and the Hobby Horse

Raggedy Ann & Raggedy Andy
Meet the Hobby Horse

It was a cool, bright summer morning, and Raggedy Ann and Raggedy Andy were resting in the shade of a giant maple tree.

Suddenly they heard a strange noise. *Clippity-clop, clumpity-clump.* Then it stopped, and they heard a loud sob and a very sad sigh.

And there, right before the Raggedys, stood a wooden Hobby Horse with big tears rolling down his cheeks.

"Don't cry so," said Raggedy Ann. "Tell us what the trouble is and we'll help you."

"I have run away from Banzan the Magician, who made me," said the Hobby Horse. "He is very mean, and beats me with a willow stick.

"Now he is chasing me," the Hobby Horse said between sobs. "And he will take me home and beat me again. Please help me, whoever you are, for you seem kind and gentle."

"Of course we will help you," said Raggedy Ann. "I am Raggedy Ann and this is Raggedy Andy. We shall not let Banzan get you."

Suddenly they saw someone coming up the path. It was Banzan the Magician. "There you are, you wicked little Hobby Horse," Banzan said. "What do you mean by running away? If you don't come with me right now, I shall beat you again."

Raggedy Ann stepped forward and said, "Raggedy Andy and I will not let you beat the Hobby Horse. He does not want to live with you anymore."

But Banzan would not give up so easily. He tried to pull a branch off the giant maple tree, but the old tree held fast to its limbs. He finally found a stout stick on the ground.

"This will make you change your mind," he cried. "Let go of my Hobby Horse or I shall beat you all!"

All this time, a redbird had been chirping a message to all her woodland friends. Suddenly, a troop of animals came marching in.

Before he knew it, Banzan was surrounded.

He held up his stick and said, "Skippety-skip, trippety-trip, now you are a magic stick! Now beat upon the woodland animals!"

He waited for the stick to work, but nothing happened. His magic was not strong enough against the goodness of the Raggedys and their friends.

The Hobby Horse neighed with pleasure.

"Maybe when you decide to do good things for others, your magic will be stronger," Raggedy Ann said.

Banzan, knowing that his magic had failed him, angrily turned and ran out of the forest.

"From now on, I shall stay with you," the Hobby Horse told Raggedy Ann and Raggedy Andy. "For I know I can stay with whomever I like best."

The Magical Boat

Raggedy Ann, Raggedy Andy, and the Hobby Horse became the best of friends.

One day as they walked through the deep deep woods, they met a fat little man dressed in a white suit and hat with shiny brass buttons.

"Hello," the little man said to them. "I am the Captain."

"The captain of what?" Raggedy Ann asked.

"The captain of the magical boat," he answered. "And I am looking for passengers. Would you three like to sail with me?"

"Oh yes, we would," Raggedy Ann cried.

"But there is no boat!" said the Hobby Horse. "How can we sail without a boat?"

"Naturally the boat would not be here," said the Captain. "A boat must be in the water. Just follow me."

So they all walked down the path through the woods until they came to the little magical boat.

It was a beautiful, shiny white boat.

Once everyone was aboard, the magical boat glided out over the smooth waters of the river.

"We will just let the boat sail in any direction it wishes." The Captain laughed. "Then we shall be surprised when we sail into an adventure!"

"What is this switch?" asked Raggedy Andy.

On the switch were the words UP and DOWN, STRAIGHT AHEAD, BACK, AIR, and WATER.

"This switch makes my magical boat even more special," the Captain said.

"For with it, we can sail the boat on the water or up in the air!"

"Can we try it?" Raggedy Ann asked. "I would love to fly in the air."

When the Captain pointed the switch to AIR, the boat rose from the water. Then it went sailing up into the sky and flew through the air, high above the earth.

The Lost Sailor

Far down below them they could see the lovely green of trees and grass, while great fleecy clouds floated by.

The Captain looked out over the sky with his spyglass.

"My goodness!" he cried. "There's a man in a tiny little boat out there. And he's waving his arms at us!"

The Captain steered the magical boat right up to where the man sat in his tiny rowboat. Then the Captain and Raggedy Andy helped him aboard.

"Gracious!" the man said as he sat down. "That's the first time I've ever been shipwrecked up in the air! I thought I would never be rescued. I'm very glad you happened to sail by this way."

"I imagine it might be lonely up here," said Raggedy Andy, "but it is truly beautiful as well. We have never seen such wonderful sights in all our lives."

Everyone was hungry, so they sat down for a feast of lamb chops, hot dogs on buns, big red tomatoes, and ice cream sodas.

Then the Sailor told his story.

"I was rowing my boat last night, when all of a sudden it began to whirl around and around. I snuggled down and closed my eyes. And when I opened them, there I was, way up in the middle of the air!"

"You must have been caught in a waterspout!" said Raggedy Andy.

"Well, here we are, landing on the earth again!" the Captain cried, and the boat went bumping down onto the ground, sending everyone flying onto the deck.

"I shall have to land a little more carefully next time!" The Captain laughed.

"Thank you very much for rescuing me," said the Sailor, and he waved good-bye as he headed back home.

And Raggedy Ann, Raggedy Andy, the Hobby Horse, and the Captain sailed on for another adventure.

Mr. & Mrs. Granny

They sailed on until they saw an old lady and an old man sitting on a log crying.

"What is wrong?" the Captain asked.

"We are Mr. and Mrs. Granny," said the old lady. "Two mean Witches came to our house, took everything we had, and drove us away."

"If you show us where these Witches are, we shall make them give back all your things," said Raggedy Ann.

So the Grannys climbed into the magic boat.

When they came to the Grannys' house, Raggedy Ann went to the front door. A Witch poked out her head and yelled, "Go away!" Then she shut the door.

"I know," said the Captain. "I'll go to the back door, and scare them out of the house." And off he ran.

Soon the other Witch stuck her head out. "Well, now we have captured your friend. Unless you wish to be captured too, you had better leave."

"What shall we do?" Raggedy Ann cried.

"Let's hide until the Witches go out," Raggedy Andy said. "Then we can rescue the Captain."

Soon, one of the Witches popped up the chimney. Then the other Witch came out the door.

"Witch Wiggle, do you see anyone?" she yelled up to the roof.

"No one, Witch Grundy," Witch Wiggle yelled back.

Then they jumped onto their magic brooms and flew off.

The Raggedys climbed into the house, and looked all over for the Captain, but they could not find him.

They sat down in a pair of rocking chairs to think. The Raggedys didn't know that these were magic chairs, and the two fell fast asleep.

When the Witches returned, they were surprised to find that they had captured the Raggedys without even trying.

The Witches laughed. "Soon we will have the magical boat, too!"

A Little Night Mischief

While the Raggedys were sleeping, the Witches tied them up and put them in a trunk.

When the Raggedys awakened, they had no idea where they were. All they could hear was the sound of the Witches laughing.

Soon it became quiet, and the Raggedys knew that the Witches had gone to sleep.

Meanwhile, the Hobby Horse and the Grannys were still hiding outside, waiting for the Raggedys to return.

"Oh dear," Mrs. Granny said. "What shall we do?"

"Mr. and Mrs. Granny!" a voice called.

Suddenly, an odd little man appeared, dressed in brown.

"It's our friend Mr. Brown!" Mr. Granny cried.

Mr. and Mrs. Granny told Mr. Brown the story of the mean Witches and about the Raggedys and the Captain.

"Well," said Mr. Brown. "We shall just have to fool those two Witches.

"You wait out here," Mr. Brown said to the others. "I'll work a little mischief of my own."

Mr. Brown sneaked into the house, and saw the two Witches fast asleep. Suddenly old Witch Grundy sat up in bed. "Listen!" she cried.

"What is it?" Witch Wiggle asked. "No one knows that the Raggedys are tied up in the trunk or that the Captain is hidden in the matchbox. So go to sleep!"

A few minutes later, something hit Witch Wiggle on the head. "Why did you hit me?" she asked Witch Grundy.

"I haven't touched you!" Witch Grundy replied angrily. "Now go back to sleep!"

But as soon as they closed their eyes, something hit them both on the head!

"There's something in this house!" the Witches howled. They jumped from their beds and raced out the door.

They spent the rest of the night sitting on a log, wondering what had happened.

The Hobby Horse to the Rescue

Once the Witches were gone, Mr. Brown found the Raggedys and untied them.

Mr. Brown explained who he was, and told them how he had scared off the Witches.

"But where is the Captain?" asked Raggedy Ann.

"I heard the Witches say they used their magic to make the Captain so small they could stuff him into a matchbox," said Mr. Brown.

So they looked and looked until they found the matchbox, and tucked inside was the little Captain.

"I can make him his right size," Mr. Brown said as he took out a magic horse-shoe nail from his pocket and rubbed it.

And there stood the Captain.

"My goodness!" The Captain laughed as he stretched all over. "I thought I would never be rescued from that matchbox."

Just at that moment, in came Mr. and Mrs. Granny.

"But where is the Hobby Horse?" asked Raggedy Ann.

"He went back to the boat for something to eat," said Mrs. Granny.

"Here he comes now!" cried the Captain.

And up he trotted. "I'm sure glad I was hungry," said the Hobby Horse.

"Whatever do you mean?" asked Raggedy Andy.

"Well," he explained, "there I was, enjoying a little snack, when who should appear but the two Witches!"

"Oh, my!" said Raggedy Ann.

"Well, I just gave them both a kick, and they went flying out the door! They were so frightened that they ran screaming off through the woods, and I don't think they'll be coming back."

"Hurray for the Hobby Horse!" cried Raggedy Ann.

All too soon it was time to leave and Mr. Granny gave the Raggedys three magical gifts from their house.

There were tears in everyone's eyes as they said good-bye. For, as you know, it is always hard to leave good friends behind.

Raggedy Ann & Andy
in the Snow White Castle

Prince Muggles

Raggedy Ann and Raggedy Andy were riding through the woods one day when they met a man named Muggles. Muggles had a bagful of magic charms that he had been using to play mean tricks on everyone around him.

"Everything annoys me," said Muggles. "I wish I could find happiness, but I know it is too late."

And much to the Raggedys' surprise, he began to cry.

"Once you make up your mind to seek happiness, it's never too late," said Raggedy Ann as she wiped his eyes.

"Is that really true?" Mr. Muggles asked.

"Yes, it is," the Raggedys answered.

"Then show me how, and I will do anything you ask," Muggles promised.

"All right," said Raggedy Ann. "First, throw away your magic charms, for you don't need them. You have more wonderful charms right in your own heart."

After Muggles threw his charms into the brook, Raggedy Ann wished for ice cream cones for all of them.

When they finished eating them, Muggles told the Raggedys his sad story.

"Somewhere in the woods," he began, "stands the beautiful white castle where my brother and I grew up.

"One day an old woman came to the castle and offered to sell me a bagful of magic charms. I thought it would be wonderful to have all my wishes come true, so I bought them.

"At first I had fun doing harmless magic tricks for all the people in the castle. But then I began to become jealous of my brother.

"You see," Muggles continued, "there was a beautiful princess who often visited the castle. She had a magical Golden Ring that she used to wish for good things for everyone around her.

"I fell in love with her, but, unfortunately, so did my brother.

"The princess and my brother were married, and when my father died, they became King and Queen.

"I was filled with envy, so I used the charms to work magic upon them."

"What did you do, Mr. Muggles—I mean, Prince Muggles?" Raggedy Ann asked.

"I wished that they would turn into an old man and an old woman, and forget all about each other." Prince Muggles cried.

"But I must have fallen asleep, for when I awoke I could not find the castle. And I never found out what happened."

"I bet your magic worked against you," Raggedy Ann said.

"Yes," said Prince Muggles. "And I will never be happy until I can undo all the wrong that I have done to the ones I love most."

"Maybe if we all look together, we can find the King and Queen and the Snow White Castle," said Raggedy Andy.

And so they set out through the deep deep woods.

The Kind Knight

They searched and searched, but they could not find anything. Soon they came to a clearing, where they sat down to think.

All at once they were startled by a big, booming voice. "You'd better get out of here as quickly as you can!"

"Who says so?" Raggedy Andy asked.

"I say so," said the voice, and out walked a Knight, dressed in armor.

The Knight waved his sword in the air, and Prince Muggles and the Raggedys ran behind a tree.

The Knight tried to run after them, but his armor was so awkward and heavy that he tripped and fell backward. There he lay with his feet in the air, crying for mercy.

Prince Muggles helped the Knight sit up. Then Raggedy Andy unscrewed the Knight's helmet and lifted it from his head.

"Mercy me," said the Knight. "I do hope no one was hurt!"

Raggedy Andy picked up the Knight's sword. "It is made of rubber!" He laughed.

"Of course it is," the Knight replied. "You see, a mean old witch has hired me to capture people who come by. But I never capture anyone, I just scare them off."

"Then why do you stay here?" Raggedy Ann asked.

"Well, I used to work at a beautiful castle, but one day it just disappeared. So

I came to work for the witch."

"What was the name of the castle?" asked Prince Muggles.

"The Snow White Castle," said the Knight.

"Well, I am Prince Muggles," said the Prince.

"Nonsense!" cried the Knight. "Prince Muggles is a young man."

And so Prince Muggles told the Knight his sad story.

"Maybe I can help you find the Snow White Castle," said the Knight. "I think I know where there might be a secret passageway. Just follow me!"

The Beautiful Castle

They all followed the Knight through the woods until he came to the foot of a great tree. There, hidden under a clump of ferns, was a large stone slab.

The Knight lifted the stone like a door, and everyone went inside.

They soon found themselves in the most beautiful place they had ever seen.

All about them was a lovely lawn where birds and animals stood frozen like statues.

And in the distance, with its red roofs and turrets almost touching the clouds, was the beautiful Snow White Castle.

When the Raggedys turned to Prince Muggles, they saw that he had become a young man. But he, too, stood like a statue.

"Well," said the Knight, "it really was Prince Muggles after all."

"Yes," said Raggedy Ann. "But why doesn't he move?"

"I don't know," the Knight replied.

They all helped carry the Prince to the castle.

When they entered the throne room, they saw a handsome man and a beautiful woman sitting like statues upon their thrones. "It is the King and the Queen!" said the Knight.

The Knight placed Prince Muggles on a seat beside them.

Although the Raggedys tried to awaken everyone, not a soul stirred. "Now what shall we do?" Raggedy Ann asked.

"We must search for the Golden Ring!" said the Knight.

"Oh, yes," said Raggedy Ann. "Prince Muggles told us about the Queen's magical ring."

"Maybe it's in the Queen's pocket," suggested the Knight.

Raggedy Ann looked in the Queen's pocket, and sure enough, there it was.

"I shall make a wish," Raggedy Ann said.

The room was very quiet; then everyone began to stir, and soon they all came to a full awakening.

The Gift of the Golden Ring

The Queen and the King and the Prince all crowded about Raggedy Ann and Raggedy Andy.

"We shall never be able to thank you enough," said the Queen.

"And we will make the brave Knight a Duke for helping us," the King declared.

"And, Raggedy Ann, you shall have my magical Golden Ring for your very own!" the Queen proclaimed.

"Thank you very much!" Raggedy Ann said. "I shall make a wish that upon every spot where we met with an

adventure, a tree shall grow with hundreds of shining magical Golden Rings upon every limb.

"And when someone with a kindly heart comes along, all he has to do is shake the tree, and a magical Golden Ring will fall down."

"This will all come true," Raggedy Andy said, "for Raggedy Ann's wishes are kindly and generous and unselfish."

The Queen was so happy that she planned the finest ball that anyone outside a fairy story had ever seen.

The brave Knight was now officially a Duke, and he danced with all the lovely

ladies of the court. And the King danced with Raggedy Ann.

What a lovely time they all had!

The Raggedys would have liked to stay longer with their friends at the Snow White Castle, but they knew it was time to return home.

Raggedy Ann and Raggedy Andy kissed and hugged everyone good-bye, and were soon on their way.

"What have you done with the Golden Ring?" Raggedy Andy asked.

"Just before we left, I slipped the ring back into the Queen's pocket," Raggedy Ann told him. "For with the Wishing Pebble I have inside me, we have enough good luck and magic. Now we have even more, because we have shared it with people we love."

Short Stories

The Picnic

"Marcella's taking us on a picnic tomorrow!" Raggedy Ann said to the dolls about their owner.

All the dolls gathered around. There was Frederika and Henny, the Dutch dolls; Uncle Clem, the Scottish doll; Cleety, the clown; the French doll with the yellow curls; and Rosa and Sarah, the pretty dolls with china heads.

And then there were the Raggedy Animals— Sunny Bunny, the Little Brown Bear, and Eddie Elephant.

"She's taking all of us?" Henny asked. "Even the Raggedy Animals?"

"Of course," Raggedy Ann replied.

"I don't see why she would want to take *them*!" Henny growled. "They're not even dolls!"

"The Raggedy Animals are just as good as any of us dolls," Raggedy Ann reminded him.

"And I'd be ashamed of myself if I were you, Henny," said Uncle Clem.

With that, Henny shuffled off to sit behind the toy box in the corner and sulk.

That night, Marcella's daddy gathered up all the dolls and piled them on the rear seat of the car. Then he went back into the house.

"I do hope Henny behaves himself tomorrow," Raggedy Ann said.

Raggedy Andy laughed. "I guess he will, because Henny won't even be at the picnic! He was left in the nursery, pouting behind the toy box."

"It serves him right, too!" the French doll said. "That's what happens when one is selfish."

The Raggedy Animals were sitting together quietly. They were all feeling very sad.

When all the other dolls had fallen asleep, the three of them climbed out of the car.

As they ran across the yard, they met Hairy Puppydog.

Eddie Elephant told him all about Henny.

"Even though Henny was rude to us," he explained, "we still want him to go on the picnic."

"Even if he did not want us to go!" Sunny Bunny added.

Hairy Puppydog had an idea. He barked at the back door until he was let into the house. Then he ran upstairs to the nursery, picked up Henny, and dropped him out the window to the ground below, where the three Raggedy Animals were waiting.

Then they all ran back to the car.

Bright and early in the morning, Marcella's family started off for their picnic. Marcella sat in the back seat with all her dolls. But she held Eddie Elephant, Sunny Bunny, and the Little Brown Bear right in her lap.

"I'm so glad you thought to bring the Raggedy Animals, Daddy!" Marcella said.

Raggedy Ann winked at Henny, as if to say, "Isn't it more fun when we share our happiness with others?"

And Henny made up his mind that thereafter he would love the Raggedy Animals just as much as he loved all the dolls.

Squeakie

Marcella and the dolls were all very excited. Today was the day they were moving down to the seashore.

"The moving men will be here soon, so you must all help me get ready," Marcella told them. "We must pack everything nice and neat so nothing will get lost."

While Marcella was packing her things away, the dolls could hear the moving men tramping around the house.

"I must go downstairs now," Marcella said as she left the room, "but I will be back to get you all before we leave."

Soon the moving men came up to the nursery. All the dolls were sitting in a row against the wall, where Marcella had put them.

The men did not know that Marcella would want the dolls to ride in the back seat of the car with her. So all the dolls were packed away in the toy box and loaded into the truck.

By the time Marcella realized what had happened, the moving men and the truck had left.

The trip to the seashore was very short, and Marcella tried not to cry.

When they arrived, the men were already unpacking.

Daddy told them how upset Marcella had been.

"We're very sorry we separated you from your family," one of them said to Marcella.

"But we have a surprise for you," the other man told her. "Last month we found this lost doll, and we've been saving it until we could find the kindest girl to adopt it."

And he handed Marcella a funny little wooden doll.

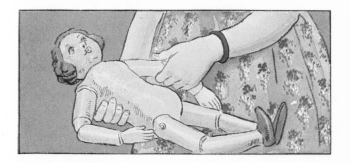

Marcella named her Squeakie, because she was made of wood, and her arms and legs squeaked when they moved.

Much of the paint on Squeakie's face had been nicked off. Her pretty clothes were all torn and dirty, but Mama offered to wash and mend them.

That night, when Marcella had gone to sleep, the other dolls gathered around Squeakie's bed. "We are so glad the moving men found you," Raggedy Ann said.

"Were you lost for a very long time, Squeakie?" Raggedy Andy asked.

"A very long time!" Squeakie replied.

Just then Daddy tiptoed into the nursery. "This is to be a surprise for Marcella," he said to the dolls, as he winked. Then he picked up Squeakie and carried her out of the room.

A few hours later, Daddy came into the nursery and put Squeakie back in bed. Then he crept out of the room.

"Squeakie! How lovely you are!" Raggedy Ann said softly.

"Daddy's  painted you all pretty and new!" Raggedy Andy cried.

All the dolls were happy. And what made them feel even better was knowing how happy Marcella would be when she woke up the next morning.

"Shipwrecked"

Marcella loved to bring her dolls down to the beach to play.

Today there was a cool wind blowing, so Marcella gave them each a ride in her little toy sailboat.

Raggedy Ann and Squeakie were the last ones to get a ride. Marcella was pulling the boat along the beach when all at once the string came untied, and the little boat, and its two passengers, began to sail away from the shore.

Marcella ran back to the house for help.

"I'm afraid we'll have to wait until Daddy comes home," Mama said sadly.

By the time Daddy got home, it was much too dark to go out in the boat. "I promise we'll get up bright and early in the morning and hunt for them," Daddy told Marcella. "Now you'd better get some sleep."

After everyone else had gone to bed and the house was quiet, the dolls got out of their beds.

They tiptoed out of the house and down to the beach, where they met Hairy Puppydog.

"Do you know of a way to rescue Raggedy Ann and Squeakie?" Raggedy Andy asked him.

"I wish I did," Hairy Puppydog sighed.

"I have an idea!" Cleety cried. "Marcella has a tin steamboat in the garage and I know it runs very fast in the water!"

The dolls ran to the garage, where they found the toy steamboat. They carried it down to the beach.

"I'm afraid only Cleety is small enough to fit," Uncle Clem said. "He will have to go by himself."

So Cleety climbed onto the little steamboat and sped away.

Cleety soon came upon a wild duck. He asked her if she had seen his two friends. But the duck was so frightened by the sight of Cleety and the boat that she flew off without answering.

So Cleety sailed on.

All at once Cleety spotted Raggedy Ann and Squeakie in the little sailboat.

"How glad we are to see you, Cleety!" they said.

Cleety tied a string from the sailboat to the steamboat, and they headed home.

Hairy Puppydog and all the dolls were waiting on the shore.

Raggedy Ann and Squeakie hugged everyone.

"Now you must all hurry upstairs and get into bed just as Marcella left you!" cried Raggedy Ann.

"Aren't you coming?" Henny asked.

"Oh, no!" Raggedy Ann laughed. "What would Marcella and Mama and Daddy think if, after we have been sailing out on the water all night, they should find us back in our beds?"

The next morning, Daddy and Marcella got up very early to hunt for the two dolls.

Imagine their surprise when they saw the little sailboat perched on the sand, with Raggedy Ann and Squeakie sitting aboard!

A Kitty Trick

Raggedy Ann and Raggedy Andy were sitting beside Looking Glass Brook when all at once they heard kittens crying.

"I wonder if a family of little kittens has wandered into the deep deep woods and is lost," said Raggedy Ann.

"Let's walk through the bushes and see if we can find them," Raggedy Andy said.

The two Raggedys walked through the high bushes toward where the kitties seemed to be.

But when they reached there, they found that the cries of the kitties came from a clump of pussy willow trees.

"I'll bet it was the pussy willow meowing!" said Raggedy Andy.

"Do you really think so?" Raggedy Ann asked. "I didn't know pussy willows made any noise!"

"Neither did I," said Raggedy Andy. "But I know the sound came directly from here."

Just then the meowing stopped.

"Someone must be playing a joke on us!" said Raggedy Andy.

"Meow! Meow!" came the cry again.

Looking closely, they saw little sharp eyes laughing down at them through the leaves.

The Raggedys sat down and laughed, for they both knew who it had been.

"Come on down," called Raggedy Ann. "You played a funny joke on us that time."

Down flew Kitty Catbird and her two friends, Charlie Catbird and Katrinka Catbird.

"You sounded just like real kitties crying," Raggedy Ann said.

"We cry like kitties to frighten off other birds who might want to harm us," Kitty Catbird explained.

Kitty and her friends fluttered around the Raggedys.

Raggedy Ann, knowing that the Catbirds were hunting for goodies, wished for a table filled with everything nice to eat.

Then they all sat down and shared a very special feast.

The Fairy Ring

How pleasant it was for the Raggedys to walk through the deep deep woods and hear and see fairies and all the other magical creatures as they went.

Raggedy Ann and Raggedy Andy stopped at a great big tree and watched a band of fairies playing in the soft, velvety moss beneath it. These were very tiny fairies, and they were as dainty as flowers.

The ten little fairies formed a ring and danced hand in hand. They whirled around in a circle, faster and faster, growing more airy as they danced.

Soon the Raggedys could only see a hazy white smoke in the shape of a ring.

They rubbed their hands over their shoe-button eyes as the smoke disappeared, and with it all signs of the tiny fairies.

All that remained was a circle of tiny mushrooms.

Just then the Fairy Queen appeared. "I see you have been watching the fairies dance," she said.

"Yes, we have," said Raggedy Ann, "and they were beautiful."

"But where did the mushrooms come from?" asked Raggedy Andy.

"I will tell you," said the Fairy Queen. "The fairies leave a circle of mushrooms so that everyone who finds it may know that fairies have been dancing in a fairy ring."

"How wonderful!" said Raggedy Ann.

"And since you are so good and kind to the woodland creatures," said the Fairy Queen, "I am going to give you one fairy wish."

The Raggedys wished for a whole week of beautiful spring weather for everyone.

"That is a nice wish, because it is an unselfish one," the Fairy Queen said. "And almost every unselfish wish in the world comes true, whether a fairy makes the wish or not!"

Ice Cream Sodas for All!

Raggedy Ann and Raggedy Andy were sitting under a tree drinking an ice cream soda with two straws.

They were so busy enjoying their soda that they did not know anyone was in back of them until someone said in a very gruff voice, "What are you doing there?"

Raggedy Ann and Raggedy Andy jumped to their feet so suddenly that they overturned their glass, and the ice cream soda spilled all over the ground.

"You've made us spill our ice cream soda!" said Raggedy Andy.

"Whatever is an ice cream soda?" the little creature asked.

Raggedy Ann and Raggedy Andy looked at each other in surprise. "You mean you've never

tasted an ice cream soda, Mr. Whatever-your-name-is?"

"The name's Skeezer," the little creature said, "and no, I've never tasted one."

"Well then," said Raggedy Ann, "I will wish for us each to have our very own ice cream soda."

"My!" exclaimed Skeezer as he felt the cold glass in his hands.

"Just wait till you taste it," said Raggedy Andy.

"Mmmm," Skeezer said, as he drank up.

Just then the Raggedys looked up and saw Scootie Squirrel in the tree. "Won't you join us for an ice cream soda?" Raggedy Ann asked.

"I've never had one," Scootie replied. "Is it really good?"

"Mmmm," Skeezer said again.

So Raggedy wished for an ice cream soda for Scootie, and another one for everyone else.

"It's just like a nice picnic!" said Scootie.

"And do you know what the best part of the picnic is?" asked Raggedy Ann. "It's sharing something you love with someone else—like an ice cream soda!"

Two Soft Brown Eyes

"The deep deep woods is such a wonderful place!" said Raggedy Andy.

"Yes, indeed," Raggedy Ann replied softly. "The farther we walk into it, the more lovely things we see."

As they looked into a clump of ferns, they saw two great, soft brown eyes looking out at them.

"Hello, my friends," a gentle voice said.

The owner of the two great brown eyes was Mama Deer, and there beside her were two of the sweetest wobbly legged baby deer you could ever hope to see.

The baby deer were so very pretty that Raggedy Ann and Raggedy Andy could not keep from petting their spotted coats.

"Why do the baby deer have these pretty spots on their coats?" asked Raggedy Andy.

"I'll tell you, Raggedy Andy," explained Mama Deer. "When baby deer are little they are called fawns.

"The fawns are taught to remain perfectly still when I leave them to hunt for food.

"I always hide them in places where the sun shines through the leaves,

because then the sun makes spots upon whatever is underneath, just like the pretty spots on my babies. And should any creature look at the place where I have hidden the fawns, though the creature may be looking right at them, he thinks it is just the sun shining through the leaves and making the spots."

"How wonderful!" Raggedy Andy said.

"I'm going to wish that your two babies grow to be nice, big, lovely deer like you," said Raggedy Ann.

"Why, thank you, Raggedy Ann," said Mama Deer.

Then the Raggedys put their arms about each other and walked away through the deep deep woods, their heads filled with so many happy thoughts!

WORTH GRUELLE

Hinkie-Dinkie

One fine fall day, the Raggedys were sitting in the meadow with Grampy Hoppytoad.

"Would you like to hear a story?" Grampy Hoppytoad asked.

"Oh, yes, please," said both Raggedys eagerly.

Grampy took a puff of his pipe, and began the story:

"I usually get pretty drowsy when it begins to grow cold. Sometimes I go to sleep right outside. And that is what happened to me last winter. I just fell asleep in the middle of the road.

"When I awakened, I didn't know where I was. I was in front of a cozy fireplace, wrapped in a nice, soft blanket. When I looked up, there stood Hinkie-Dinkie."

"Who's Hinkie-Dinkie?" asked Raggedy Andy.

"Well," said Grampy Hoppytoad, "everyone said that Hinkie-Dinkie was a mean magician who would change you into a different creature if you got near his house.

"So I said to him, 'What are you going to change me into?'

"And Hinkie-Dinkie said, 'Mercy me, Grampy Hoppytoad, Mother Nature made you a Hoppytoad and that's what you'll always be!'

"And he laughed so cheerily that I knew he wasn't fooling me."

"How did you get into Hinkie-Dinkie's house in the first place?" asked Raggedy Andy.

"Well, Hinkie-Dinkie found me fast asleep on the ice-cold path and carried me to his home.

"And do you know, Hinkie-Dinkie took care of a whole houseful of poor little creatures?

"Well, when I told all the meadow creatures about Hinkie-Dinkie saving my life, no one dared to think anything bad about him again."

"What a wonderful story, Grampy Hoppytoad," Raggedy Ann said. "And it just goes to show that so many, many people are really kind and good when we get to know them."

The Fairies' Cure

It was a bright and sunny day as Raggedy Ann and Raggedy Andy wandered through the meadow. Suddenly they came upon Carlie Canary, who was looking quite sad. He was holding one of his feet close to his body as if it pained him.

"Have you hurt your foot?" asked Raggedy Andy.

"Yes, I have," Carlie Canary said. "There is a sharp thorn stuck right into it!"

"Let us see if we can pull the thorn out," said Raggedy Ann.

Carlie Canary flew over and perched on Raggedy Ann's open hand.

Raggedy Andy found two little flat pieces of wood, and by holding them together like tweezers, he was able to pull the thorn from Carlie Canary's foot.

"Oh, my, that feels so much better!" Carlie Canary chirped.

"And now I will give you a magical cure," said Raggedy Ann, and she kissed Carlie Canary's foot.

"That was truly a magical cure!" Carlie Canary cried.

"And I know where that magical cure first came from," said a tiny voice, and suddenly a little Gnome appeared. "Would you like to know?"

"Oh, yes, we would," cried the Raggedys.

"Well," said the Gnome, "a long time ago the fairies gathered together and decided to find a cure for all the little hurts that children seem to get.

"So the fairies made a very magical sweet medicine and they put it on the lips of everyone, especially every mama and daddy in the world. Then, all the mamas and daddys would have to do is to kiss the spot where their little one hurts, and that will be the cure.

"And that is why kisses cure," the little Gnome told Carlie Canary and the Raggedys. "And that magical present is worth more than all the gold and precious stones in the whole world."

The Brownie's Kiss

Raggedy Ann and Raggedy Andy loved to wander through the Happy Meadow.

As they walked along Looking Glass Brook one fine day, they stopped to admire a row of yellow-red lilies nodding in the sunshine.

They were surprised to see a little creature spring from the ground and gently touch each of the flowers.

"Why did you touch each lily?" asked Raggedy Andy, who was always quite curious.

"Do you mean to say that you did not see what I did?" the little creature laughingly asked.

"Maybe you were too quick for our shoe-button eyes," said Raggedy Andy.

"Then watch again!" The little creature laughed, and again sprang up and touched each lily.

"Now I see!" Raggedy Ann sang out.

"So do I!" Raggedy Andy chimed in. "There is a tiny brown spot on every lily just where you kissed it!"

"And now I know what you are," Raggedy Ann said. "You are a Brownie! And we have always wanted to meet a Brownie!"

"Well, now you have met one, and I am pleased to have met you, too," the Brownie replied.

But Raggedy Ann was still full of questions. "Do you leave a brown spot wherever you touch anything?"

"Oh no!" the little Brownie answered. "I leave a brown spot only when I kiss someone I like very much."

"How happy all the children will be to learn this!" exclaimed Raggedy Ann.

"But why?" Raggedy Andy asked, somewhat puzzled.

"Oh, Raggedy Andy, just think of all the children who have freckles and are unhappy about them!"

"Oh, now I see!" Raggedy Andy cried, and jumped up and down for joy. "Every little freckle is a sign that a Brownie has kissed a child he loves!"

The Hootieowl Party

Grandma and Grandpa Hootieowl lived in the hollow trunk of a large beech tree. It was a very cozy place in which to live, for it was always nice and dry inside.

One day, Grandma Hootieowl saw the two Raggedys coming through the deep deep woods.

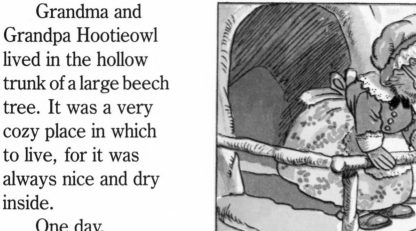

"Won't you come up and visit with us?" she asked. "It looks like rain, and we are very cozy up here!"

"Thank you very much!" the Raggedys replied.

Grandpa Hootieowl dropped his little rope ladder, and Raggedy Ann and Raggedy Andy climbed up to the Hootieowls' home.

"What would you like to have with your tea?" asked Grandma Hootieowl.

"We do love ladyfingers and cream puffs," said Raggedy Andy with a smile.

Grandma Hootieowl looked bewildered.

"Dear me," she said. "I've never even heard of those things."

"I have an idea," said Raggedy Ann. "Why don't you and Grandpa Hootieowl sit down and rest while Raggedy Andy and I make you a surprise."

"What a nice offer," said the Hootieowls, as they sat down in their most comfortable chairs.

Raggedy Ann wished for ice cream sodas and sandwiches and cookies and doughnuts and ladyfingers and cream puffs. And Raggedy Andy helped to serve the feast.

My! Weren't Grandpa and Grandma Hootieowl surprised when they tasted all of those good things.

And while they were eating, Raggedy Ann quietly made another wish. She wished that the Hootieowls' organ would play music all by itself. And it did!

The music could be heard all through the woods, and soon all the woodland creatures were gathered at the Hootieowls' house for a wonderful party.

Mr. Muskrat & Timothy Turtle

One fine day as the Raggedys walked along Looking Glass Brook they came upon Mr. Muskrat standing in the water and digging a hole in the bank.

"Whatever are you doing, Mr. Muskrat?" Raggedy Ann asked.

Mr. Muskrat laughed. "Someone has come and filled my doorway with pieces of mud and grass!"

"Who could have done that?" asked Raggedy Ann.

"Well, when I saw these pigeon-toed tracks, I knew it was Timothy Turtle!"

"What will you do with Timothy Turtle when you catch him, Mr. Muskrat?" Raggedy Andy asked.

"Timothy Turtle is a funny fellow," Mr. Muskrat said. "He always plays a prank on someone and then he walks away a few

feet, pulls his head into his collar, and falls asleep and forgets all about what he has done."

Just then Timothy Turtle came walking pigeon-toed around the bend.

"Well, here you are hard at work, Mr. Muskrat! Building a new house, I suppose?" Timothy Turtle said as he sat down.

Mr. Muskrat winked at the Raggedys. Then he went inside and came out with four slices of bread and jam.

Timothy Turtle soon finished eating. "Guess I'll swim out to the log and take a nap," he said. Then he walked down to the water.

"You see!" Mr. Muskrat laughed. "He has forgotten all about his prank!"

"I think it is so nice that you forgave him," said Raggedy Ann.

"Oh, there was nothing to forgive!" Mr. Muskrat replied. "For I love to work, so if Timothy Turtle got some fun out of it, then I don't mind. For I have the fun of undoing what he did."

"You're right, Mr. Muskrat," said Raggedy Ann. "And think how much happier we would all be if we could just learn to look for the fun in our work!"